For Lilia,
WHO ALWAYS LOVED SOUP

BEAR and CHICKEN

by Jannie Ho

RP|KIDS
PHILADELPHIA

One very cold day, **BEAR** was hungry from his morning walk when . . .

he saw a *chicken*, frozen in the snow!

How does one defrost a *chicken?*
thought **BEAR**.

BEAR burrito-wrapped *Chicken* in his favorite blanket.

Chicken woke up to the sound of a hot, crackling fire. BEAR smiled . . .

but all *Chicken* saw were his
SHARP TEETH.

"Hello, there," said **BEAR** as he reached for

his cookbook. "You are just in time."

In time for what? *Chicken* thought.

101 WAYS TO COOK

BEAR brought over a huge pot.
It was so big that *Chicken* could . . .

FIT INSIDE!

BEAR filled it with water and turned on
the stove. The water boiled.

Chicken simmered in suspicion.

Chicken peered into the pot,

took a step away,

only to **CRASH!** right into some herbs.

"Yes, basil!
Chicken, that is perfect."

BEAR began sharpening his knife.
Onions, *chop*. Carrots, *chop*. Celery,
CHOP CHOP.

"Hmmm . . . what else is missing?" said BEAR.

He looked over at *Chicken.*

"Chicken, come a little closer and smell
the delicious soup," BEAR said.

"It's almost time for *lunch*."

She wiggled her tail feathers,

tripped on a potato,

and jumped off the counter.

Knocking down everything in sight,

Chicken ran with all her might!

Chicken zig-zagged through the trees,
but soon **BEAR** closed in on her.

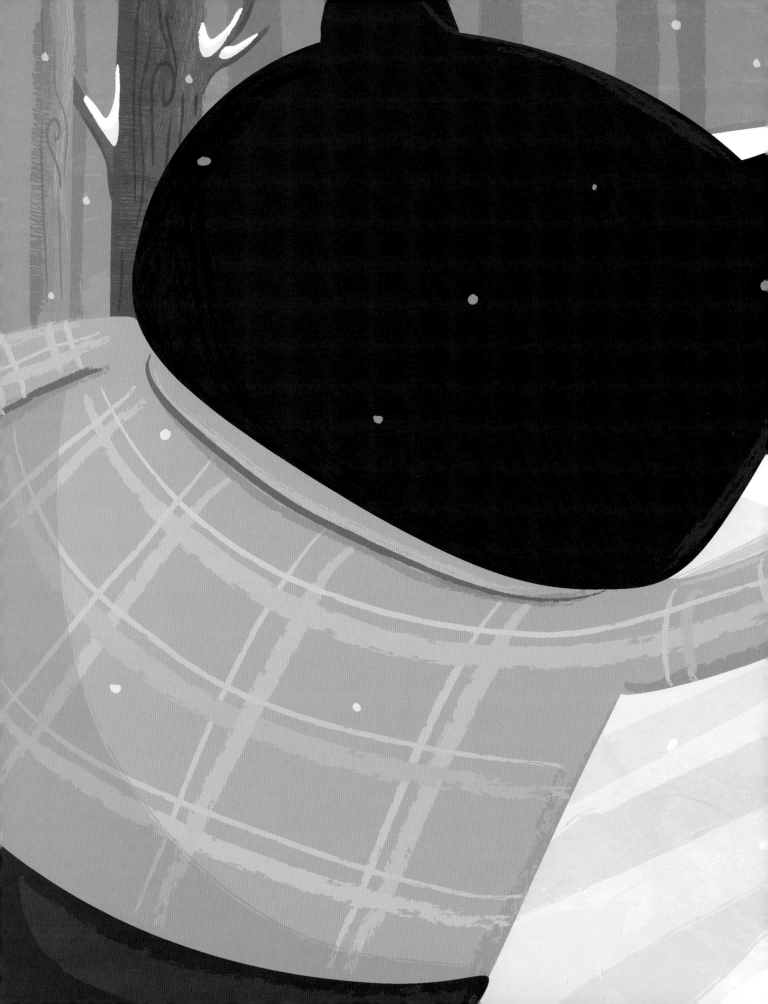

"This is the end!" *Chicken* squawked.

"I'm Chicken Soup!"

"Where are you going?" huffed **BEAR**, catching his breath. "You forgot this."

"You're not going to eat me?" *Chicken* asked.

"Eat you? I was making lunch . . .
for the both of us," **BEAR** explained.
"Aren't you hungry?"

"Nope, not hungry at all."
Chicken shook her head. Then . . .

RRRRRUMBLE!

Chicken's tummy
GROWLED.

"So you *are* hungry after all." **BEAR** chuckled.
Chicken began to laugh, too.

"Will you help me find my way home?"
Chicken said as she rubbed her tummy.

"After some lunch?"

"Yes, after lunch," **BEAR** agreed.

The two new friends walked back to **BEAR**'s cabin,
where a big pot of *vegetable* soup
was waiting for them.

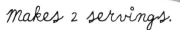

BEAR'S VEGETABLE SOUP

makes 2 servings.

YOU'LL NEED:

Be sure to ask a grownup for help whenever you are cooking in the kitchen!

1 onion, minced

1 teaspoon vegetable oil

1 carrot, chopped

1 potato, peeled and diced

2 tablespoons tomato paste

½ teaspoon salt

2–3 tablespoons fresh basil, chopped

¼ teaspoon oregano

2 cups water or vegetable stock

1 stalk celery, chopped

¼ teaspoon black pepper

HERE'S WHAT YOU DO:

1. Heat the oil in a pot over medium heat. Add the onion and sauté for 1 minute, stirring frequently.

2. Add the carrot and celery, and sprinkle in the salt, pepper, and oregano. Cook for 2 to 3 minutes. Stir in the potato and sauté for 1 minute.

3. Pour in the water or vegetable stock, add the tomato paste, and bring to a boil. Reduce heat to low and cook, stirring occasionally. Cook for 15 minutes or until vegetables are tender. Stir in the basil and heat through.

Now you are ready to share your soup with a friend—chicken, bear, or kid!

A Note about Black Bears
(for kids and fearful chickens!)

Black bears are only found in North America and mainly live in forests. They are mostly vegetarians with their diet made up of grass, leaves, wild berries, nuts, seeds, and insects. Black bears have a great sense of smell and will travel far to find food, sometimes entering into campsites and garbage bins. They are not picky eaters!